LITTLE LAMB
BAKES A CAKE

by Michaela Muntean · pictures by Nicole Rubel

Dial Books for Young Readers

E. P. Dutton, Inc. New York

Little Lamb wanted to make a
birthday cake for her mother,
and she wanted it to be a surprise.
But where do you begin when you
want to make a cake?

"I believe you begin with a recipe,"
said Little Lamb, so she looked in
the cookbook and found a recipe
for yellow cake.

Find the card with the picture of the cookbook.
Put it on the box with the number **1**.

Little Lamb read the recipe.
Then she looked in the refrigerator
and the cupboards.
There was a little bit of everything
but not enough of anything to make a cake.
So Little Lamb made a list of what
she needed.

Find the card with the picture of the shopping list.
Put it on the box with the number **2**.

Little Lamb took her list to the grocery store and rolled the metal cart up and down the aisles.

Flour, baking powder, milk, eggs, butter— soon she had the ingredients she needed to make a cake.

Find the card with the picture of the ingredients.
Put it on the box with the number **3**.

When she got home, Little Lamb took
the groceries out of the bag and set
them on the counter.

"Oh dear!" she cried. "I forgot to
buy sugar, and without sugar my cake
will not be sweet."

So Little Lamb went next door and borrowed
a cup of sugar from Black Sheep.

Find the card with the picture of the cup of sugar.
Put it on the box with the number **4**.

Quickly Little Lamb mixed all the
ingredients together in the biggest bowl she
could find, spilling just a little bit
of everything.

Then Little Lamb greased and floured
two round cake pans.
Very carefully she poured the batter
into the pans.

Find the card with the picture of the cake pans.
Put it on the box with the number **8**.

"Now my cake is ready to bake,"
said Little Lamb.
She put the pans in the oven
and waited until the batter had baked
to a golden-brown color.

While the cake was cooling on a rack,
Little Lamb made pink frosting.

Find the card with the picture of the oven.
Put it on the box with the number **9**.

She frosted the layers, and on the
top of the cake Little Lamb made
four yellow flowers.

Oh, Little Lamb's mother was going to be
very, very surprised!

Now turn all the cards over, one by one,
to make a surprise picture.